TRiCKSTERS

Rigby, is an imprint of Pearson Education Limited, a company
incorporated in England and Wales, having its registered office
at Edinburgh Gate, Harlow, Essex, CM20 2JE.
Registered company number:872828

www.rigbyed.co.uk

Rigby is a registered trademark of Reed Elsevier,Inc.licensed to
Pearson Education Limited

Tricksters first published 2002

Series editor: Wendy Wren

11
14

Tricksters   ISBN 978 0433 07696 4
Group Reading Pack with Teaching Notes ISBN 978 0433 07702 2

Illustrated by Sarah Warburton, Toni Goffe, Lyn Stone
Cover illustration © Korky Paul 2002
Repro by Digital Imaging, Glasgow
Printed and bound in China(CTPS/14)

CONTENTS

Cunning Jack

by
Martin Waddell

Once upon a time, a long time ago,
there was a boy called Cunning Jack.
How did he get that name? Well, he
took on a band of robbers and came off
best, because of his cunning.

The robbers attacked the poor farmer
that Jack worked for. They beat the
good man and left him lying dead.
They went off with his money and all
his bony beasts.

That left Jack without a job. The poor farmer's widow was left with no money and no beasts she could sell, and a young daughter to care for.

"What shall we do, Jack?" sobbed the widow. "The neighbours can't help us. The robbers have taken their money too. All the people are scared of what they'll do next."

"I'll go after the robbers and get your money back!" cried Jack. He said goodbye to the widow and set off to find the robbers' hideaway.

He found the robbers' hideaway. It was a dark house, deep in the woods.

"Please, Sir, I've seen what you do and I like it," Jack said to the Robber Chief. "Will you make me a robber like you?"

The Chief laughed and said, "No one would be scared of *you*. No one would hand over their money to *you*. Go away!"

That night, Jack came back with a small bit of wood that he had shaped like a pistol. He chose a spot down the lane from the robbers' house. He put on the widow's cloak and stood on a tree stump. The cloak hung down over the tree stump so that Jack looked like a giant.

Jack waited until one of the robbers came by with a bag full of jingling coins that he had just stolen.

"Drop the money, or I'll shoot you dead!" shouted Jack.

The terrified robber
dropped his bag and
ran away to the house.
"There's a giant robber
out there with a huge
pistol. He stole my
money and he scared me
almost out of my life!"
he told the Robber Chief.

The robbers came roaring out of the house to tackle the giant and . . . Jack came up the lane to meet them. He was just an ordinary size. He was not wearing the cloak and he did not have a bit of wood shaped like a pistol, but he did have the bag of money.

"Now I've proved I'm a robber like you!" Jack said, and he gave the money bag to the Robber Chief.

"You must pass my test first," said the Robber Chief. "I'll send one of my robbers down to the market to steal a fat sheep. You must steal the sheep from him on the way back."

"That's easy!" said Jack.

The next day, the Robber Chief sent one of his robbers down to the market. The robber was on his way back through the wood with the sheep when he saw a shoe on the road.

"Now there is a good leather shoe," thought the robber, "but it's not much use on its own." He walked on past the shoe with the sheep. He walked on round a bend in the road— and there was *another* shoe, just like the first one.

"It's my lucky day!" thought the robber. "If I go back for the first shoe, I'll have a pair of new shoes!" He tied the sheep to a tree and ran back to pick up the first shoe.

The robber came back with his new shoes. The rope was still tied to the tree, but the sheep was not tied to the rope.

Jack had run off with the sheep!

"That silly sheep ran away from me," the robber explained when he got back to the house.

"Is that so?" said the Robber Chief. "It must have been a fast sheep! Go back to the market and steal me another one! Make sure you bring it back with you this time!"

When the robber had gone, Jack showed up with the sheep.

"I've passed your test," he told the Robber Chief.

"Not so fast, Jack," said the Robber Chief. "You've played some kind of trick but that doesn't make you a robber. I've sent for another sheep. Steal that one too and I promise you can be a robber in this gang."

Well, Jack tricked the robber again!
The robber came back up the track
with the second sheep.

"Baa–baa!" baa-ed Jack from behind a
tree in the wood. "Baa–baa! Baa–baa!"

"That must be the sheep I lost
yesterday!" thought the robber. He tied
the new sheep to a tree and went to
look for the lost sheep.

He could not find it. When he came
back from the wood, the new sheep
had gone too.

"I've lost another one!" the robber told the Robber Chief, when he got back to the house.

"Go away!" the Robber Chief roared. "You're too stupid for me!"

When Jack showed up with the second sheep, he got the job as a robber.

The next day, the widow came weeping to the robbers' house.

"Chase that crying woman away, Jack," said the Robber Chief. "I don't want her sobbing all over me!"

Jack came out of the house with a big knife in his hand. "Did you do as I told you?" he whispered to the widow.

"I did!" said the widow. "I've a bag of red berry juice hidden under my cloak."

"Take that!" said Jack and he stuck the knife in the bag.

"You've killed me, Jack!" wailed the widow and she fell to the ground.
A pool of red spread around her.

"I've killed her for you," Jack said to the Chief. "Now I've proved I'm as bad as you are."

"I don't mind killing a farmer or two," said the Robber Chief, "but killing widows could get us into a heap of trouble."

"Hmmm. . . that's true," said Jack. "Perhaps I'd better magic her back to life with my magical stick."

Jack pulled out a stick. "Watch this," he said to the Robber Chief. He waved the stick over her head and the widow sprang up and ran away.

The Robber Chief quaked with fear at the thought of a magical stick that could waken the dead from their sleep.

"It could kill you if I asked it to," Jack told him. "I will make it kill you, if you don't do what I say. You know my stick works so you'd better do what I tell you."

"Don't kill me, Jack!" begged the Robber Chief. He shivered and shook and sobbed on his knees. "I'm no match for you."

"I'll let you live," said Jack, "if you give me all the money you stole and – "

"And what?" wept the Robber Chief.

"You must all go away, and never come back!" said Jack.

That was the end of the robbers.

All the people who had been robbed got their money back and Jack married the widow's daughter. He worked hard and became a rich man with six fields and six cows and six sheep and six goats and six children as well.

So that is how Cunning Jack earned his name, and he used his wits to help his friends for the rest of his life.

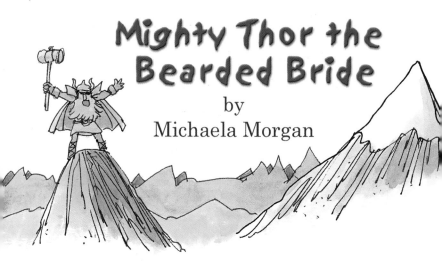

Mighty Thor the Bearded Bride

by
Michaela Morgan

Long ago and far away in the land of
the Viking gods, the gods were very
angry and unhappy – and they were all
blaming Thor.

"I'm sorry," he wailed. "I didn't mean
it to happen."

Thor was famed among the Viking
gods. He was famous for his mighty
strength. He was famous for his huge
appetite – but, above all, he was famous
for his magic hammer.

Thor protected himself with this
magic hammer. He protected all the
other gods, too.

He had fought many a fierce giant with that hammer.

He had terrified many a troublesome troll – but now the hammer was lost.

"One of our greatest treasures – lost!' sighed Freya, the goddess of beauty. "How could this happen?"

Little by little, the story came out: Thor often ate far, far too much. He often drank far, far too much. When he felt fat and full of food, he just had to lie down and sleep. And as he lay snoozing and snoring, the King of the Frost Giants had sneaked away with the magic hammer.

"I've got to get it back!" wailed Thor. "But how?"

"I've got an idea!" said Loki, the god of mischief.

"What is it? I'll do anything," promised Thor.

"And we'll all help," added Freya.

"Good!" said Loki. "I will need both of you to help to make my plan work."

Loki explained. "I've been speaking to the Frost Giants and I know that their King will return the hammer – on one condition." He took a deep breath and looked at Freya. "On condition that he can have Freya as his bride!"

"No! NO!! NOOOOOO!" shrieked Freya. "I will never marry a hairy old Frost Giant! I can't! I shan't! I WON'T! You can't make me!"

"Oh, you must," urged Thor. "We must all be ready to do anything to get the hammer back. I need it to protect us all."

"I won't," said Freya. "Not for all the hammers in heaven! I won't do it!"

"Just listen to me," Loki said to Freya. "You won't really marry him. In fact, you will never even meet him. We shall send someone dressed in a bridal gown to look like you. Someone who will be let into the King's hall and can then grab the hammer and bring it back."

"Well, that's better," sighed Freya.

"Brilliant!" said Thor. "I knew you'd think of something. Now, who can we dress up as a bride?"

"You!" said Loki.

"Me!" cried Thor. "What! How? No! Never! IMPOSSIBLE!" he thundered.

Freya shrieked with laughter. There wasn't a Viking god in the place that wasn't giggling, or sniggering, or laughing out loud.

Thor stamped his enormous foot. "How can I dress up as a bride? Look at me!" Thor was huge. He was a mountain of a man. When he walked, the earth shook. When he came to a river, he just waded across. His voice roared like thunder and his eyes glowed as red as coals. His beard was wild and red.

"Impossible!" said Thor.

The other gods looked at him and agreed. He would not make a very beautiful bride!

Loki explained. "It has to be Thor," he said. "The hammer is very heavy and Thor is very strong – and the hammer knows its master. Thor is our only hope of getting it back and… " he looked at Thor, "you did say you'd do anything to get it back."

Thor slumped in his chair and sulked.

"We will dress you in a big dress," said Loki, "and a veil, a thick veil – a very thick veil," he added, looking at Thor's bearded face.

"B-b-but..." blubbered Thor, "they won't believe I'm Freya."

"When we've dressed you up and put Freya's special jewels on you, they will," said Loki.

"B-b-but... I won't know what to say!"

"I'll go with you," said Loki, "and I'll speak for you. You just stay quiet, and look pretty – as pretty as you can anyway," smiled Loki.

"B-b-but…" blubbered Thor, and then he broke into a final desperate wail. "I'VE GOT NOTHING TO WEAR!"

"Leave that to me," said Freya, and she went off to find cloth and ribbons. Soon she was back with curtains and bedspreads, ropes and tassels, and in no time at all she'd made a reasonably good wedding dress.

"I'm keeping my trousers on under it," insisted Thor.

"All right," said Loki. "Keep your trousers on."

"I'm wearing my own boots, too, " added Thor.

"You'll have to," said Freya. "No ladies' shoes were ever made in your size. Now let's do something with your hair. Would you like curls – or some plaits? Bunches, maybe?"

Thor sighed. Loki threw a thick veil over Thor's head and Freya added the finishing touch, her very special necklace.

"When they see this necklace, they are sure to think the bride is me," she said.

"Right, let's get this over with," growled Thor, and he picked up his skirts and strode off.

"Walk more slowly," begged Loki. "Try to look a little bit lady-like. Take smaller steps ... don't bellow ..."

But Thor was already on his way, bellowing and thundering, thumping the ground with his big, booted feet, his veil streaming behind him and his long skirt hooked up over his arm.

A message had been sent and the Frost King was waiting for his bride. A fine feast had been prepared and Thor's magic hammer was proudly displayed behind the King's throne. Everything that could be done had been done, to welcome the beautiful new bride.

The doors burst open and in strode Thor with Loki skipping alongside, whispering, "Take daintier steps!"

The King saw his bride arrive, and exclaimed, "She looks like a fine, strong girl!"

"Hurrumph!" said the 'fine, strong girl'.

"Ssh!" whispered Loki.

"Freya, my dove, my beauty, my love, will you dance with me?" asked the King.

"No!" Loki cried, quickly. "Freya is tired after her journey. Just let her sit quietly."

"A little refreshment, perhaps?" suggested the King and he handed a plate, heaped with meat, to Thor.

Thor grabbed it and scoffed the lot.

"My bride has a fine appetite," gasped the King.

"Ah," said Loki, "she hasn't had a bite to eat since she heard she was to be married. She's been too excited to eat. Now she's very hungry."

"A little drink, my dear?" asked the King, and he offered a jug of wine. Thor took the jug and drank the lot. He banged the jug back on the table, wiped his mouth and burped. The sound echoed round the hall.

The King looked astounded, but Loki whispered, "She hasn't had a drop to drink for days. She longs to be your wife without delay."

"Her face seems rather red," muttered the King. Through the thick veil, Thor's beard and eyes glowed like hot coals.

"Blushes," said Loki. "Never has a bride been so excited. Let's have the marriage at once. She can't wait to be your wife."

The King was flattered. "Let us be married at once!" he said.

"Give us the hammer first," said Loki.

Servants struggled to carry it to them. As soon as it was within reach, the 'bride' grabbed it, swung it around 'her' head and, with a wild yell, jumped on the table. Then Thor, the 'bride', was off, leaping over people, sliding through food, whooping and yelling out the door, with Loki running after.

As Thor ran past, his veil flew to one side and the King glimpsed his face. The Frost King gasped and then fell silent.

Soon Thor and Loki were back with the other gods. Loki was happy that his plan had worked. Freya was very happy to see her necklace again, and Thor was even happier to have his wonderful hammer back.

Back at his court, the Frost King was the happiest of all. He was still sitting in a puddle of wine and squashed food, rubbing his eyes and gasping, "Imagine... imagine... I almost married THAT!"

Tops and Bottoms

by

Jan Mark

Tam had a farm and he kept it well. There were no weeds in his wheat, no stones among his turnips. He worked all day, from dawn till dark, and went home to supper with Mary, his wife.

Each year, at harvest time, the farmers held a reaping match to see who could cut the most corn, and Tam won every time, fair and square.

"How do you do it, Tam?" the other men asked.

"Hard work and Mary's cooking," Tam replied.

At last Tam won so many reaping matches that he saved enough money to buy more land. He chose a field with a deep, damp ditch along one side of it. While Tam was standing there, deciding what he would plant in spring, someone climbed out of the ditch.

Now, Tam had honest dirt on his hands, but the person from the ditch was dirty all over, and dressed in the kind of tattered old rags that Tam put on his scarecrows.

Tam knew at once what had climbed out of the ditch, and he was not pleased. It was a boggart.

"What are you doing on my land?" the boggart said.

"This is my land," Tam said. "I've just paid for it, fair and square."

"Who did you buy it from?" the boggart said.

"I bought it from the parson," Tam said.

"I was here before the parson," the boggart said. "I was here before the church. I've been here for ever and ever, and this is my land."

"Then it's a pity you didn't take better care of it," Tam said. "Look at these stones and thistles."

The boggart began to jump up and down. "It's my land and I'll do what I like with it."

"We'll see about that," Tam said, leaving the boggart jumping up and down in the ditch.

After supper, Tam said to Mary, "There's a boggart in my new field, and he says it belongs to him."

Mary said, "That's bad, that is. But try to keep him happy, husband. Tell him you don't mind sharing."

Next morning Tam went back to his field and the boggart was waiting in the ditch. When he saw Tam, he sprang out shouting, "Get off my land!"

"I've been thinking about that," Tam said. "Why don't we share it, half and half? You dig and I'll dig, you sow and I'll sow, you weed and I'll weed, you reap and I'll reap."

"I have a better idea," the boggart said. "You dig and I'll watch, you sow and I'll sleep, you weed and I'll whistle, you reap and I'll eat."

"I need to think about this," Tam said, and went home to Mary. The boggart dived into the ditch and laughed a nasty laugh.

"Don't worry, my love," Mary said, when Tam got home. "Boggarts are bone idle and very, very stupid. Tell him you'll dig, sow, weed and reap, and offer him half the crop, tops or bottoms."

Back went Tam to the field by the ditch and out came the boggart. "Get off my land!"

"How about this?" Tam said. "I'll dig, sow, weed and reap, and whatever comes up we'll share, half and half."

"That's more like it," said the boggart.

"Wait a minute," Tam said. "Which half do you want, tops or bottoms?"

"Bottoms," the boggart said, and went back into the ditch.

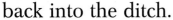

All that year Tam worked in his fields. He sowed cabbages in one, beans in another and, in the field by the ditch, he planted wheat. When the seeds were sown, he scared away the birds. When the plants came up, he hoed out the weeds. When no rain fell, he carried water from the well to keep his crops alive – and, all summer long, he never saw hide nor hair of the boggart.

But when it was harvest time, Tam sharpened his scythe and went to the wheat field. At once, the boggart leaped out of the ditch.

"Have you come to cut the crop?" the boggart said. "Don't forget my half."

"I haven't forgotten," Tam said. "Bottoms, wasn't it?"

"It was," the boggart said, and settled down to watch Tam work, smiling a toothy smile.

Tam smiled too.

All day, Tam went up and down his field, cutting the wheat and binding it into sheaves. When evening came, the boggart said, "Now I'll take my half."

"Not so fast," Tam said. "Your half's still in the ground. Bottoms you wanted, didn't you?"

There was nothing the boggart could do. He had asked for bottoms and bottoms were what he had got, the roots of the wheat. Tam had tops, the grain and the straw.

Tam and Mary were happy that winter and the boggart stayed sulking in his ditch, but when spring came and Tam went out to the field, the boggart was waiting.

"Do you want to share again?" Tam said cheerfully.

"You don't catch me out twice," the boggart said. "This year I'll have tops."

"Fair enough," Tam said.

The boggart went back to his ditch to sleep the spring and summer away, while Tam sowed his crop and weeded and watered it. All year the boggart waited for the wheat to be ready but, when he woke up and looked at the crop, he saw that Tam had planted turnips this time.

Along came Tam with a spade.

"Tops, wasn't it?" Tam said, and started to dig. When the field was cleared, Tam had a fine pile of turnips and the boggart had nothing but withered greens.

Next spring the boggart was ready and angry when Tam came to the field.

"This year, we'll do things properly," the boggart said. "There'll be no more tops and bottoms, we'll have one side of the field each, half and half."

Tam went home to tell Mary.

"You must plant wheat again," Mary said. "Then go to my brother, the blacksmith, and ask him to make you a hundred iron rods, as thin as wheat stalks. When the wheat comes up, I'll tell you what to do."

All year, the boggart slept in the ditch, while Tam worked. At harvest time, Tam got up early and stuck the thin iron rods among the wheat stalks on the boggart's side of the field. As the sun rose, he picked up his scythe.

"Oy, boggart! Time to cut the wheat!"

The boggart climbed out of the ditch.

"We'll have a reaping match," Tam said. "Winner takes all. Fair enough?"

"Fair enough," the boggart said. He picked up his own scythe, and the two of them started work. Tam's blade went through the wheat as easily as cutting butter, but the boggart's scythe soon grew blunt on the iron rods.

"Stop a bit," the boggart said. "I have to sharpen my blade."

"Oh, no you don't," Tam said. "In a reaping match we all sharpen our scythes at the same time."

"And when will that be?" the boggart said.

"Oh, not till noon," Tam said and kept cutting.

"Well, that's me finished, then," the boggart said, for his scythe was as blunt as a pig's backside. He threw it down and jumped into the ditch and Tam never saw hide nor hair of him again.